VISITS

G. D. Spilsbury

ERGAMOT

for Ralph and Catherine

Visits

IT WAS A CRISP APRIL MORNING in the Schuylkill Valley, the landscape marked by the long ridges of the Appalachian highlands, still a soft brown with winter's trees. Ellie Miller stood in her father's childhood bedroom in her grandparents' house where the front windows faced this peaceful view. The back windows, in contrast, came up against the town's tallest mountain, its steep incline fragrant with untouched woods. So much silence filled the room, for the stucco cottage perched on a terraced wedge above Egelman Road, whose macadam swath had also been carved from the mountainside. The Millers' house had been built in the early 1900s by previous owners. Fruit trees and tangled remnants of a kitchen garden grew in a patch of yard on one side of the house. On the other side was the kitchen door with sixty brick steps to the street and a grassy slope that stopped abruptly at the garage's rooftop—the garage itself a dugout in the hillside. Honeysuckle covered its roof, sending out an intoxicating fragrance as one passed by on the steps.

Low boxwood bordered the pathway, exuding a strange pungency that Ellie never forgot and recognized ever after.

It was seven o'clock on Saturday morning. Ellie opened one of the windows that overlooked the front lawn that descended to a narrow plateau and goldfish pond, supported by a stone retaining wall from the street. Daffodils' spiky leaves shot up around the pond's rim, their tight yellow heads not yet open. Birds chirped merrily, for winter was over, despite early spring's capricious weather that included occasional snow, so wet it melted instantly, refreshing the earth and air. Ellie listened for a moment to the birds' spirited activity, their delight in being able to hop freely from tree to tree—winter's hunkering down in frozen bushes finally over. Their exuberance touched her heart, bringing a smile to her lips, despite the sadness and preoccupation of her grandfather Earl's impending death. He lay downstairs on a hospital bed in the dining room facing the sylvan mountain view from the picture window, but it was his last view, his last hours or days to see it, to see life, his life in the only town that had been his home.

For weeks now, the dining room had been a makeshift hospice where Ellie's red-headed grandmother, Lillian, also slept on a rollaway bed. The pastoral valley with its border of mountains had been desecrated in the 1960s with tract housing filling the flat basin. Luckily, it was possible to keep one's gaze above that ugly intrusion and see only

Pennsylvania's serene beauty that never failed to transport the spirit to a higher realm.

Ellie quickly washed up and went downstairs. In the front hall, through the dining room's dark wood archway, she could see that her grandparents were still asleep. She tiptoed to the kitchen, with its old-fashioned wallpaper, linoleum floor, and permanent smell of toast and coffee. Everything was exactly the same as in her childhood when she came for summer vacations with her parents and older sister, Laurie. Many of Ellie's first memories and sensations lived in these walls and on the steep hillside outdoors—like sitting in a washtub on the grass, Laurie in a tub beside her, the two of them blowing bubbles from plastic pipes, Ellie less successful than her more capable sister. Each effort got closer to producing one of Laurie's big iridescent globes that soon popped, sending them into belly laughter. The men—Grandpa and their father, Dave—stood watching, faces intent on the little tots chortling in innocent fun and discovery. Two fathers who loved children. On each visit, Ellie and Laurie made a ritual roll down the front hill, their arms tight around each other to travel as one. Screaming with the thrill of danger, they flung themselves apart just before touching the fish pond's edge—Grandpa guarding them with a worried brow, at the ready to pull them from the water if they miscalculated. Best of all, as Ellie grew and gained more independence, she loved exploring her grandparents' home office—a narrow, dank room off the kitchen with metal file cabinets and desk drawers filled with curiosities. It was the world of business, of clients and records, of pens, pencils, receipt books, and a typewriter. Only now, at age twenty-three, did she realize that in that dark room—for it backed up against the mountain—she had come upon her destiny: the world of print. She liked desks, working at desks, she liked offices that produced printed results. Before she could write paragraphs, she made stapled books of drawings that told the stories in her mind. When she was twelve, her father gave her his Underwood typewriter when he bought an IBM Selectric. She put it to immediate use, loving the clack-clack of the keys as they produced professional-looking letters and words. She loved the sound of the carriage return's authorial conviction. After college, she got a low-paying job on a neighborhood rag, doing whatever the mom-and-pop owners needed— errands, calls, deliveries, research, but it didn't pay the bills and she had to waitress at night.

Ellie put the coffee on and a few minutes later, Lillian came into the kitchen through the dining room's swinging door. Her curly red hair and round, plump face looked sleepy. She wore a faded floral robe that zipped up the front of her short, soft body.

"Good morning, dear," she whispered lovingly, reaching up to give Ellie a kiss. "Did you sleep all right?"

Ellie nodded with a smile. She was familiar with Lillian's first hour of the day—when she padded around in a state of peaceful half-consciousness, her personality free from its childish traits that would surface later: resentment, grudges, and suspicion. Ellie had first sampled her narrower side around age four, when she played with Lillian's costume jewelry. The jewelry was another tradition the sisters had when they visited. Piles of it lay on Lillian's bureau top like an open treasure chest. Gleefully the girls decked themselves out with strands of necklaces, tinkling bracelets, and clip-on earrings, but always under Lillian's tense surveillance, for she didn't like sharing her possessions. On this occasion, Laurie was downstairs playing checkers with their grandfather in the cozy kitchen booth with its green vinyl seats and formica table. Ellie was suddenly on her own without her big sister directing their play. Her mother and grandmother stood by as her unschooled hands grabbed up necklaces.

"Put them down!" her mother said harshly.

Shame and fear instantly burned Ellie's cheeks—shame for being scolded in front of her grandmother and fear at the warning tone in her mother's voice. In reflex, she giggled with high-pitched silliness and grabbed a fake pearl neck-lace. She dangled it at the them as if to say, "Look at this one, let's play with this one!" It was her child's way of attempting to distract them from her misdemeanor and to win back her good-girl status.

But her mother grabbed her by the arm, and twisting it up lifted her away and banged her down roughly on the wooden chair by the door. Waves of panic cut off Ellie's breath—what would her mother do next? What worse punishment lay in store for her? Her hand still held the fake pearls, but unknowingly, for fear possessed every particle of her.

But her mother left the room abruptly. Instantly Ellie's grandmother filled her place, her face bending close to Ellie's to give her the meanest look, while her hand snatched away the pearls. She stalked out of the room on her short legs, blowing out a huff of disgust.

Ellie had sat on the chair for quite a while, waiting to be excused. But her mother never returned, and eventually she got up and tiptoed back to the world of the living, not sure she was allowed to liberate herself and fearful she might be punished for it. She wanted nothing more than to find Laurie, hide behind her taller figure, feel her sisterly protection. Laurie, two years older, was her partner in self-preservation from their mother's unpredictable rages.

"How's Grandpa?" Ellie asked, returning her mind to the present and smiling at her grandmother. She generally accepted her grandmother's mercurial moods and behaviors and steered away from triggering them. Overall, she knew Lillian had a good heart, however mistrustful, miserly, and on occasion downright mean. Her dark sides were much the same as everyone else's.

"All right, things being what they are—he's sleeping now. He has so much phlegm and no more strength to cough it up."

"I heard him. I feel so bad for him."

"But he doesn't have pain, darling. When he cries out like that, it's not because of pain, it's his liver—his liver isn't right."

He had howled periodically throughout the night, a wounded animal in the wild left to die. And he was dying. Whenever Ellie stood next to his bed and met his large brown eyes, so alive in his gaunt face, her mind struggled to grasp that instead of being bedridden to get better, he was bedridden to die. And he knew it—he knew with those trapped brown eyes that he was waiting for life to shut down his consciousness.

"Did you find the coffee, dear?" Lillian asked absent-mindedly, moving around the room, opening drawers and shuffling their contents, then opening the basement door and bending over a tall tin can on the steps that housed pretzels and other happy-hour snacks. But she wasn't looking for anything in particular. She was just shuffling about while her internal motor warmed up for the day.

"Yes, it's just starting to percolate."

"Good."

Lillian pushed through the swinging door to the dining room, leaving it open. Ellie could hear her straightening up the table's surface, now littered with pills, lubricants, and other hospice-care items. Her job was nursing these days and she was good at it, having grown up in an era lacking modern medicines. She knew how to use herbs for common illnesses and pain. She had nursed her mother through death and was now ready to do the same for her husband. Ellie stole a glance into the dining room. Lillian was bent over the bed, stroking Earl's forehead and cooing soothing words in her high, musical voice. "I love you, darling, I'm right here, and I won't leave you, no sirree, you have my word!"

She returned to the kitchen. "He's resting comfortably. This could go on for weeks, you know." Her tongue clucked at the prospect.

"How?" Ellie whispered. "He's emaciated. He looks like he's been in a concentration camp." Tears came to her eyes—Grandpa living in that horrible dying state and conscious of it.

"Yes, dear, but look how he's lasted—this has been going on since November."

"But he wasn't this thin—even a few weeks ago he looked different. He's just a shell now." He was all bones with loose skin hanging from his arms and shoulders—the part of him that showed above his covers.

Lillian poured coffee into two cups and added a splash of

milk to her own. "When your father was here in January, we looked for a home. The hospital said there was nothing more they could do for him. But in the end, I couldn't put him in a home. He needs to be here, with me, here in his own home."

"I'm so glad, Grandma. And so is he. Thank you."

"But your daddy, after all that work he had done! And the place he found—it was *bee*-u-tiful!" she said in her singing way. "They wanted fifteen hundred a week—can you believe it?—fifteen hundred!" Her bushy, red-and-gray eyebrows rose incredulously. "How's that possible? Why, it's highway robbery!"

"Thank God he's here, in his own home, with you."

"Yes, but if you only knew how hard your father worked to find that place."

They sat down at the booth in the cozy nook between the kitchen and the office. "Nope—I wasn't going to let that man die alone," Lillian said. "We've been together sixty years, and I'm strong, I can take this." She flexed her bicep under the robe, then dropped her arm and gave Ellie an angelic smile, eyes winking humorously. "But oh Lord, was that place your daddy found something to see!"

Ellie nodded, smiling, but her thoughts were still on her grandfather. She couldn't reconcile his death. He had meant so much to her in childhood, teaching her to roller skate and ride a bike in their spacious driveway in Philadelphia. And here at his house on the mountain, they had played checkers, chess, and gin rummy in the booth. She had listened with fascination to his bad English whenever he tossed down a card he didn't like: "That don't do me no good." She liked imitating his gruff speech when she rejected her own cards, and using his "ain't" back at him—it made them pals. He had been born out of wedlock, and his mother never married. Lillian said it was because of her lame foot, a birth defect that spurned suitors. Earl had gone to work as a boy, delivering newspapers, and after sixth grade, apprenticed with a printer. This led to becoming a journeyman and eventually a master craftsman owning his own printshop downtown. With no more than four or five employees at a given time, he produced invitations, flyers, programs, bulletins, yearbooks, and badges with ribbons that Lillian sewed on. Berks Printing Co. handled any sort of job work and prospered enough to survive the Depression and accumulate savings. Lillian was Earl's partner, endowed with her German ancestors' acumen for moneymaking. She also ran a side business selling fine china, silver sets, and cookware to couples who published their engagements in the local newspaper. She called them and promoted her wares. She also made sure these customers went on to buy their wedding invitations from Berks Printing. Earl and Lillian had expected Ellie's father to join the company after college—a local college of course. But as Dave's high school years neared their finish, he announced he intended to become a doctor. They urged him to pursue pharmacy instead—they would help him open a drugstore downtown with a soda fountain. Bewildered, they watched their only beloved son apply to famous East Coast schools and leave them forever for that sophisticated world beyond their comprehension. Fortunately, after his many years of education and training, he settled the family in Philadelphia, close enough to visit. "But oh, what a home he bought!" Lillian often trilled when the subject came up. "And my God, did you ever see so many homes like it?—one after the other like a grand parade."

The impressive mansions, built nearly a century before by wealthy Philadelphians, were beyond the elder Millers' class and taste. Nevertheless, they came every Christmas and sat stiffly on the elegant sofas, feeling out of place and disconnected from the growing grandchildren who now spent all their time with their private school friends. The days of checkers and gin rummy were over.

"When your father was here last weekend and saw his dad, he broke down," Lillian said to Ellie as they drank coffee in the nook. "I never saw him so shook up—he cried, your daddy cried. It was something."

Ellie nodded—her father crying was hard to believe. He had been brought up traditionally—"men don't cry." But the 1970s were allowing him openings to the new freedoms and behaviors granted to men, like hugging his father at the start and finish of their vacations. Before that, a strong handshake had been the manly way of expressing love and loyalty. Even Grandpa was open to the new mode of hugging his son, however stiffly and quickly. And Dr. Miller, still handsome in a dashing way, wanted to be part of the new trends, the incrowd. He grew his dark hair and silver-sprinkled sideburns like the TV celebrities and bought casual clothes for social occasions that in the past had required a jacket and tie. He wore a navy-blue turtleneck for winter ski parties and a pink, short-sleeved shirt for summer barbecues. Of course, his teenage daughters egged him on, wanting hip parents, parents who accepted sexual freedom and women's lib. By this time, the Millers had also produced their longed-for son—Dave Jr. His arrival had transformed their unfulfilled family life to lively times that revolved around the adorable baby. Little Dave—nicknamed "Jay" for junior—grew up with a happy, carefree personality nurtured unconditionally by his elders.

"He rushed out of the room," Lillian continued, glad to air the thoughts that had been bottled up in her all week. "We heard this terrible noise, and Earl cried out, 'Is that my Davy? Is that my Davy crying?'" I ran after him—he was right here, all crushed up in that corner." She pointed to Ellie's corner of the booth. "He was sobbing like I've never seen. His whole body shook. I tell you, it was something."

Ellie tried to imagine the scene of her father all balled up and crying in the nook—the man who never winced, the man who never shirked an unpleasant duty, the man who handled any crisis that arose in their family, such as Ellie's expulsion from her girls' school when she was caught smoking. He had gone in and talked to the headmaster. He had come back out with the verdict: she could return to school. Everyone looked up to him because he was a doctor. It had happened more than once that in a public place an urgent voice called out, "Is there a doctor in the house?" Dave was the one to get up and attend to the victim until an ambulance arrived. Jean was proud to be his wife, appended to him, though her face generally was less open to showing affection and love. Ellie wondered if her cold, Presbyterian upbringing had shaped this trait in her. She did liven up for parties—her chance to dress up and be admired. She loved drinking gin and tonic and laughing with others, her gaiety charming and contagious. Her beauty, too, always shone above anyone else's in the room. She was the belle of any occasion and derived fulfillment from that role.

"I said, 'Don't cry, son, don't do this to yourself.' But oh, if only you could have seen him, Ellie, how bad he hurt. I thought I'd die." Lillian pressed her hand to her heart, eyes lifting to the ceiling. "No sirree, I'll never forget him saying, 'That's my father, that's my father!'"

With a sigh, Lillian wriggled her roundness out of the booth and shuffled back to the kitchen. "A little more coffee, dear? And how about some apie cake? Or shoofly pie? I know you like shoofly pie. Remember to take some home with you." She opened the fridge. "And lookee here, I have scrapple—Habbersett's—the real McCoy."

Ellie followed her. "No thanks, Grandma, I'll make some toast. What about you?"

"Nothing for me. I might have a piece of cake later. The toaster's on the table." She pointed toward the nook.

Ellie opened the bread bin near the open dining room door. She imagined her grandfather was lying awake in there, listening to them. It felt surreal that a wall separated the realm of the living from the realm of the dying, as if her grandfather had been set aside from life, no longer part of it.

"Our pastor's been so good to us," Lillian said, refilling their coffee cups. "He came to the hospital every day and checked on Earl. I swear, that man has God in him—never misses a day visiting the sick. And let me tell you, he has a special feeling for your grandpa. Why, just the other day, when he came up all those steps just to see Earl, I saw tears in his eyes. He told me this death is real hard for him."

"He's not dead yet, and he can hear us," Ellie said quietly.

Lillian didn't answer. She turned away and padded around the room eyeing objects that might need straightening. "Yes, indeed, there isn't anyone who doesn't love Earl."

Ellie heard the resentment in her voice—his popularity being greater than hers—the usual lot of women who worked hard, who often made and upheld the foundation of a striving household.

"Sixty years we've been together, sixty, I tell you."

"It's a long time."

"You'd better believe it, kiddo." A sudden belly laugh rippled through her, and her eyes twinkled up at Ellie from behind her glasses. "And don't you go thinking it was always a bed of roses—it took a lot for us to stick together." She turned and swayed in her robe back to the nook. "Let's sit again, dearie, I'm just waking up. And it's so nice to have you here, someone to talk to."

They resettled themselves, and Ellie put her bread in the toaster. Lillian continued her morning musings. "I'm going to be honest—that's the way we are in this family—am I right?"

"Yes. We can talk."

She nodded. "It's like this, Ellie, if I could do it all over again, I wouldn't have gotten married—or not so young. I was only eighteen, and if I had waited, who knows who I might've married. But I married Earl."

Ellie smiled patiently. She had heard this story since childhood—how her beautiful grandmother from a small business family of several generations had been too good for the humbler roots of her grandfather, especially given his illegitimacy. In those days, fatherless children were stigmatized for their parents' sin.

"But oh, how he loved me!" her musical voice sang with eyes rising to the ceiling. "And mind you, I wouldn't have anything to do with him. And Earl was no plain Joe—he was something to look at! He had eyes to melt your heart. But, I said no, I refused him."

Ellie smiled teasingly at her grandmother and continued the next part of the story, for she knew it well. "But then one day, at a big picnic, he climbed a cherry tree to impress you."

Lillian let out a hearty laugh. "Don't you know it! That boy thought he could woo me with cherries, but he went out too far on the branch and it broke. I'll never forget the sound of it cracking. He landed flat on the ground and lay there like he was dead. I ran over to him and took his head in my lap. Finally, he opened those beautiful eyes of his and I felt my heart lurch. That's how it all began." She laughed. "I can't believe it's been sixty years now." She dabbed the corners of her eyes under her glasses—tears that were bittersweet. "But I tell you, honey, if I could do it all over again, I'd be free like you. Don't go and get married till you have what you want. Life's too short. I wanted a career but got married instead."

"But you had a career—you've been a successful business-woman."

"That's true, but I wanted to be an actress!" Her shrewd blue eyes shot sparks at Ellie. "Mind you, I had talent—I could sing and dance, I played the piano. I wanted to be on the stage, but my father wouldn't hear of it. He was so strict with me."

"Why couldn't you be an actress?"

"It wasn't ladylike. They were considered loose women— you know, easy for men. Papa made me work in the family business. How I hated it—we made machine parts for the local companies. I had to sit in that horrible old warehouse and do the books, day after day, only free on Sundays. And let me tell you, Ellie, that was no place for a girl. There were only men there—greasy, dirty men. They liked to pester me. They touched me, pinched me. They made rude passes— such things were allowed back then. I thought I'd die." Her round cheeks shuddered with the memory. Ellie could relate. Only recently had such gross behaviors been made taboo.

"Well, maybe in the end business inspired you—I mean with Grandpa, the two of you building your own business."

She chortled. "Damn right about that. Your grandpa and me—we worked—every day, before the sun came up and into the night. We started at the bottom and did everything ourselves—we planned, talked things over, took one step at a time, and saved. We counted every penny."

Ellie smiled. She could imagine her grandmother counting every penny. She had seen several old-fashioned change purses bulging with pennies in the top desk drawer of the musty office.

"We wanted children, but I didn't get pregnant. It was ten

years before your daddy came along, and we had already resigned ourselves to being childless. We weren't happy about it, un-uh, but I was willing to adopt. Your grandpa said no, he didn't want that, someone else's child. By the time Davy was born, we had already bought the plant and had enough savings to start investing. Later, we were able to help with his education and your first two homes. Don't forget, he was still in medical school when you and Laurie were born."

Ellie listened, understanding where her father's business sense came from—his hardworking, thrifty, American-dream parents. As soon as he had a hospital salary coming in, he too had begun to invest, mainly in real estate like his parents, but also in stocks, something Lillian and Earl wouldn't touch, having lived through the crash and Depression. They preferred certificates of deposit and government bonds. Lillian had shown Ellie a stack of envelopes waiting for their twenty-year maturity date. Lillian also cashed Earl's Social Security checks and hid the wads of bills in a paper bag behind the dining room's tall cupboard—emergency funds, she said. Thousands of dollars lay hidden there. And Lillian still sold china and silver sets to young couples. She also owned and managed summer rentals on the Jersey Shore. Work, money, saving fueled her life.

After their second cup of coffee, Ellie went into the dining room and leaned against the side rail of her grandfather's bed. Whenever he rested peacefully, she thought he might be dead. She stared down at his gaunt face, his mouth sunken without its dentures, his sharp nose distinguished. Even now—with only the rattly bones of what had once been a proud, virile man—he was handsome, strong featured, his face carved precisely with an artist's chisel. Tears rolled down her cheeks and into the crack of her lips. Earl's eyes opened and they stared at each other. She memorized his brown eyes that still shone with life—scared life—and she wondered if he was also memorizing her, before his unknown journey beyond the earthly conscious state that would physically separate them forever. What was that like, she wanted to know, to be him and aware of taking these last looks? She picked up his gnarled hand—the hand she had often studied for its capabilities despite its similarity to an ancient tree. She felt his old familiar grip—strength was still there in that wasted body that could no longer move. But the hand could still squeeze with intention. With her other hand, she smoothed back his silken white hair, rubbed his fleshless shoulders above the covers, and tried to smile. "I love you, Grandpa," she said, "you're my sweetheart." His face remained immobile but the gentle brown eyes with their shining pupils acknowledged her words. She wondered if she reminded him of her father, if her youth and the bounce to her step took him back in time, when his son would return from college, filling the house with his vibrancy—the house so silent and empty without him. The morning before, she had showered and combed her dark hair back from her face into a ponytail. Wearing pants and a flannel shirt, she had walked into the dining room with a bright smile for her grandfather. His eyes had popped in alarm, almost in fear— was it the fear of seeing a ghost? He thought I was Dave, young Dave, Ellie had thought. When he saw she wasn't Dave, his head had rolled listlessly on his pillow. What he wanted now, in his last living moments, was his son.

As Lillian moved through the kitchen and dining room, opening drawers and cabinets without an objective, Ellie went into the living room, its wood archway facing the dining room's identical one, with the front hall and stairs between. She looked around, breathing in the old empire-style furniture with faded brocade upholstery. Around the stone fireplace hung long-forgotten Christmas tree lights. They blinked when plugged in but had lost their luster to years of caked dust. The forgotten condition of the room gave it a hazy gloom, as if time had stopped there decades before.

At the far end of the room, next to her grandmother's piano, Ellie opened the closet whose shelves were chock-full of Miller memorabilia: photographs, letter packets, broken instruments, yearbooks, baby books, newspaper clippings lauding Dave's high school achievements, election badges her grandfather had printed, crochet needles and yarn, and a tiny, black leather boot with miniature buttons that had belonged to her father. For a while, Ellie sat on the couch and looked at the old photographs—her grandmother at eighteen when she was slim and comely in a soft period dress before the 1920s. A newer one showed Ellie's parents in their famous glamour, seated at a homecoming ball in the late 1940s. Her dad wore a black tuxedo that matched his black hair. He laughed confidently into the camera, his arm around his fiancée's bare shoulders. She wore a strapless satin gown that highlighted her smooth curves. She smiled, with less self-assurance than he, yet pleased to be forever captured as a good-looking couple at a fancy event. Last, Ellie looked at a photo of her grandfather in his fifties, posing outdoors in a fine suit, his posture upright and proud. His lack of an education didn't matter in his community. He was an exemplary citizen in every way.

Ellie went back to the kitchen and immediately saw a frosty brown beer bottle on the counter, her grandmother apparently not shy about starting so early. In the past, she often made a point of declaring that she never touched a drop before five o'clock, but maybe she did, or maybe the stress of Earl's decline had made her start earlier. The German Americans—the Pennsylvania Dutch—loved to make merry—it was part of their culture. Ellie's father had grown up in the community's century-old way of enjoying themselves at big meals on Sundays after church. They met at their community center high on the mountain and spent the long afternoon eating, drinking, laughing, flirting, and dancing. The children frolicked outside and came in rosy-cheeked when the mid-afternoon dinner bell rang. Everyone sat at long, communal tables and spoke their forefathers' dialect. When the band played, the kids danced too, with their friends, parents, and relatives, swinging their arms and legs to the music, their faces lit. This warm, cohesive tradition had died out after the Second World War, around the time Dave set off to make his own life, beginning with college in New England—a foreign region to his parents, whose farthest frontier was New York City. But Dave continued the merry-making of his heritage, so Ellie grew up never questioning drinking and laughing together as a positive part of life—or once the work day was done at five o'clock. At least Lillian was drinking the local brew's half-size bottles.

"Ellie, come help me with your grandfather," Lillian's chirpy voice called from the dining room. Ellie joined her at Earl's bedside. His eyes looked scared.

"He's all washed and fresh now," Lillian said. "I bathe him every day and then rub him down with nice cream. I shave and comb him, don't I, Earlie? I make you look real pretty." She bent over his face and kissed it several times in a circle. "I love you, darling, what will I ever do when you're gone?" Her croon wasn't entirely authentic, and Ellie braced herself for one of her grandmother's ploys. She didn't have to wait long.

"Isn't it wonderful to have Ellie here? She's going to help me take care of you."

With that, Lillian whipped the covers off Earl, exposing his naked, wretched body and limp penis. Ellie froze in horror at her grandmother's insensitivity and her grandfather's mortified face, his eyes instantly meeting hers. Her grandmother's mean streak had purposely taken advantage of his helplessness to violate his modesty, his personal rights to his body, his self-respect. She had acted heartlessly. Ellie didn't know how to extract herself from the situation and stood there in a state of unbreathing guilt and pain for her grandfather, and dislike for her grandmother's antics.

"Here, Ellie, take this cream and rub it into his back and shoulders," Lillian said cheerfully, as she pushed Earl to his side revealing the bones of his buttocks.

Ellie took faltering steps to the bed while her grandmother cooed over the shriveled body on the sheet. "Ellie's going to make you all soft and smooth, my darling," she singsonged. "Do his back, honey. No one's ever going to say I didn't take wonderful care of this man. Why, just look at his skin—not a blemish on it! Even the nurses at the hospital couldn't get over it. 'This man has been kept,' they said. 'Yes, indeed, this man has been cared for.' Go on, Ellie, do his back." She pushed Ellie's arm and then stepped away. Ellie squirted a patch of cream into her palm and spread it across the sharp, protruding shoulders of her grandfather's back.

The skin was indeed soft. His body was the size of a starved boy's, shivering in the nightmare of this ordeal Lillian had imposed on him. Ellie hoped her loving hands conveyed her oneness with him—the two of them separate from her. Meanwhile, Lillian moved to the kitchen door, reached inside for her beer on the counter, and took a satisfying draft. She put the bottle back and returned to the business of nursing, wiping her mouth with her hand.

"Ellie's making you look real pretty, sweetheart. She'll always have this moment to remember, helping Grandma take care of you. You'll always have this, Ellie—you'll be happy for it someday." She unceremoniously shoved Earl to his other side. "Not on your life could I put this man away," she crowed. "No home could care for him the way I do. In the hospital, they never bothered to turn him. He got terrible bedsores. I wouldn't let them touch him after that. I took three buses every day to get to the hospital, because that's how I am. No amount of trouble is going to stop me. And look at him now, look how beautiful he is." She leaned over the bed, beer on her breath, and spoke to the back of his head. "You're still beautiful, you hear me, Earlie, beautiful! And I love you, darling." She kissed his hair. Surely he despised her in that moment, Ellie thought.

Finally, the trauma of morning care ended. Lillian flapped a clean sheet over Earl's wasted body and left him on his side to stare out the picture window at the abiding mountain range under a blue sky. "I'll feed him in a little bit," she said, returning to her beer in the kitchen. "But it's hardly worth it—he doesn't eat. That's what's going to get him."

"He can hear you, Grandma."

She ignored the comment but used her foot to kick the swinging door closed. Then she cut a slice of apie cake and took a bite while standing at the counter with her beer. New memories came to her. "Marie was here on Thursday. Marie was your grandpa's secretary. He took her out of the orphanage and helped her through school. They were devoted to each other. He can't talk anymore, but when Marie came in and he saw her, he cried out, 'Marie!'—just like that, 'Marie!'" Lillian's blue eyes shot darts at Ellie. "Did you hear me? He loved her. I saw it—the way he looked at her." Her plump hand lifted the beer bottle for a sip. "But I'm not jealous. I'm not that type. I'm happy Earl and Marie were so close."

Ellie nodded, feeling glad her grandfather had had Marie in his life, however intimate or platonic, and she imagined the latter, knowing Earl's values. But this was the first time Grandma had ever mentioned her. She wondered if her father remembered Marie, and if he knew anything about this bond.

"Oh, yes, it was something when he cried out 'Marie!'"

Lillian repeated. "I'll never forget it, as long as I live. Won't you have a beer, Ellie? It's made right here. This is the only place you can get the little bottles. They aren't distributed."

"No thanks, Grandma."

"I always have my beer, but I'm careful. And these times are hard on me."

Ellie understood her subtext—for now the five o'clock rule was suspended.

"I guess I'll go up and get dressed now," Lillian said, and her rotund figure moved off to mount the front hall stairs.

Ellie sat down on a dining room chair next to Earl's bed and tried to read the book she had brought, but her sight was glazed. How could she concentrate on anything but what was happening in this house full of memories and her dying grandfather two feet away? She felt as hollow and unreal as she imagined he felt.

Lillian soon returned. She hadn't taken long washing up and putting on clothes that should have gone to the laundry pile—a brown jersey with an old spill on the front and loose polyester pants whose hemline was inches above her ankles. Her old black shoes from the five-and-dime were worn on the sides, for she walked on the outsides of her feet, with slight bowleggedness.

"I can run errands for you, Grandma," Ellie offered, following her grandmother into the kitchen. "Do you need anything?"

Lillian opened the fridge for another beer and answered from behind the door, "Once all of this is over, I'm going to look better after myself. I don't have time now. Since the fall, I haven't been to the hairdresser. I haven't left the house since Earl came home. A boy from down below comes up for the garbage and Peggy Mullen brings me my groceries. I give her a few dollars for gas. What I put up with for your grandpa! But I know it's right, what I'm doing is right."

She popped off the beer cap with a bottle opener fastened to the counter's side. "Have one, darling, won't you have a beer with me?"

"It's too early for me, Grandma, I'll have one later."

"Beer was the drink in our house growing up—it was like water or soda for us. But mind you, I watch myself, and I never drink too much." She poured some of the beer into a small glass and shuffled toward the nook. "Let's sit again, I want to talk. I'm alone most of the time." She put down the glass and bottle and reached way up to hold Ellie's face between her palms. She pursed her lips for a kiss, and Ellie bent to receive it. "I'm so glad you're here, darling, it's such a comfort. We're family, we can talk."

Ellie felt glad to please her grandmother, even though she didn't know how she would make it through the day keeping her company. There was nothing in her own life—her dreams or troubles—she could share with her grandmother. And she didn't have a boyfriend to gossip about. Only family topics connected them, and Lillian repeated her pet subjects nonstop. With an inner sigh, Ellie dutifully slid into the booth.

"I tell you, if I could do it all over, I wouldn't have married Earl. It was instinct that made me do it. He was the kindest, sweetest boy I had ever met, and let's face it, that's saying a lot. But if I could live my life over again, I'd experiment like all you girls today. I only knew one man in my life, and I think people should know before they marry if they can live together. But I won't complain. Dad was good to me, we were good to each other, and we made it through. We never went to sleep on a fight. I want you to remember that, Ellie, if you ever marry, don't go to bed on a fight, always make up first. I only hope it's that way for your father. You don't know how I worry about his marriage to that woman!" Her lips twisted.

"His marriage is fine, Grandma, you needn't worry about it," Ellie said, though it was common knowledge that her grandmother had no love for "that woman," and the feeling was reciprocated.

"Really? Can I really believe you? I worry all the time. I tell your dad, 'Dave, you never laugh anymore. Why don't you laugh anymore?'" She gave Ellie a piercing look through her glasses. "You can tell me, we're family, we're close—does your mother ever give him a hug or a kiss? I never saw it." Her hand banged the table. "And look how he does everything for her! She's like a queen who thinks she deserves it! Does she ever do anything for him?"

"Of course she does—a lot!—and she loves him."

"Really? Can I believe you? I want to believe you, I want to believe there's love between them."

"I promise there is."

She shook her head. She lifted her glass and drained the sips left in it.

Lillian's words about Ellie's mother hung in the air. Ellie imagined her parents. It was partly true that her father took the initiative with her mother. When he came home from work, he opened the front door with his usual happy whistle that beckoned her. With slight reluctance, she would let herself be folded into his arms and accept his rocking, loving, sweet talk against her hair. Sometimes she would join him in his armchair to curl up in his lap, all cuddly. So she did reach out first on occasion.

Lillian poured more beer into her glass, always a few sips at a time. "We were so unhappy when your father called and told us he was getting married."

"But he was bringing you his good news."

She shook her head. "It wasn't the right time, and we told him so. We said, 'Davy, you still have medical school and all those years of training. What're you going to do if Jean gets pregnant?'"

"Which she did."

"He wouldn't listen. He knew what he wanted—her. And your other grandmother was against it too. We talked on the phone—we agreed they were too young, what with Davy having that long education in front of him. But in the end, we went along with the plan, because that's what they wanted."

She sniffed her beer as if it were brandy. "Help yourself to a beer, Ellie. Don't you like the kind I buy?"

Before Ellie could reply, a loud knocking on the kitchen door startled them. Lillian quickly hid her beer bottle and glass behind the toaster and worked her way out of the booth. "Now who could that be at this hour? It isn't even nine o'clock."

She let out a delighted cry when she saw who stood on the other side of the door's windowpane. A cluster of bells tinkled as she opened the door. "Well, lookee here, look who's come up all those steps to see us. Come in, Pastor. Ellie, come meet our pastor!"

Ellie smiled and shook hands with the pastor while Lillian bubbled on. "This is my granddaughter, Pastor, Davy's second daughter, Ellie. She's come all the way from Philly to help me with Dad. Oh, the work I have when I'm by myself! The two of us washed him down and rubbed him with cream. I'm going to feed him next, but he can hardly swallow. He had a terrible night with the phlegm. It's getting too hard to bring up."

"Well, it sure is nice of you to come and help your grand-mum," the pastor said. He presided over the stone-and-timber Lutheran church at the end of the street. He was in midlife, tall, a little bent, with nervous but friendly eyes. His tight brown curls threaded with silver coated his head evenly, and his permanent smile creased his thin face like a mask.

"This is *von*-derful that you're here, Pastor," Lillian sang out, using her Pennsylvania Dutch *V* on *W* words like *wonderful*. "It means so much to Earl. Can I give you some coffee?"

"Oh, no, nothing for me, but thank you, Lillian. I just wanted to stop by and see how Earl was doing."

She led him to the dining room. "Tell me, Pastor, did you and Diane go out for dinner last night?" She shot Ellie a glance. "Friday's his night to take his wife to dinner."

"Indeed we did—we ate prime ribs at the Ben Franklin. By golly, were they good!"

"And what a bargain! Your father went there last week, Ellie. The pastor told him about it. The prime ribs are only five dollars—big, gorgeous pieces of meat!"

"I'm afraid it won't last, once everyone finds out about it," the pastor said. "But, of course, that's what we want—prosperity for our businesses." He leaned slightly over the hospital bed. "Morning, Earl, how're you doing today?"

Earl struggled to say something but only choking sounds emitted.

"Don't worry, Pastor, he's glad you're here."

The pastor put his hand on Earl's ragged shoulder. "And, I bet my bottom dollar just being home these few weeks has made you feel like a new man. You've got Lillian's home cooking and the best nursing care in the county."

"He's not eating, Pastor. It sets off his coughing. He can't catch his breath. Why, only three weeks ago, when Ellie was here, he could still get out of bed with the two of us helping. We could walk him to the table, and he could eat dinner sitting up. He wouldn't let me feed him, not in front of Ellie. He wanted her to see he was still a man and could do it himself. Oh, Lordy, I thought there was hope."

A few more exchanges took place around the bedside until their small talk ran out. Then, the pastor straightened his shoulders, indicating it was time to take his leave.

"Well, I'd better get myself over to the hospital now, but it's sure been good to see you, Earl, and I'm glad to know these ladies are taking such good care of you. And your view—the best in town, I'd wager." He gave Earl's shoulder a farewell squeeze and then turned to Ellie with his friendly smile. "It's been a great pleasure to meet Lillian and Earl's granddaughter, and I know they appreciate your being here."

Ellie smiled back and shook hands politely. Her grand-parents' way of life was so different from her family's in Philadelphia. Here the lifestyle was old-fashioned and homey, based on community friendship and values, a connecting tissue helped by the church, something missing in the younger Millers' sophisticated city life—nor did they seek it.

"Thank you for your visit, Pastor," Lillian said, accompanying him to the kitchen door. As soon as it closed, she went to the nook for her beer and sat down. Ellie joined her, resigning herself to more of Lillian's repetitive conversation.

"Our pastor's a good man, a real friend to us. Before Earl got sick, he and his wife would come over to play pinochle with us. We'd sit right here, have a beer together, play cards. What good times! And how he loves your grandpa—this death really hurts him."

She sipped her beer and wiped her mouth. Soft peach fuzz covered her upper lip like a faint mustache. Her habit of twitching her nose and upper lip like a rabbit called Ellie's attention to it.

"Don't you know," she went on, her mind drifting to her favorite topic—Dave, her son—"your daddy's a brilliant man. Am I right? Just look at all he's done, and still in his forties. I never saw anyone work the way he does. And it's going to kill him. I don't want to be here for that, oh no, I'd rather be dead."

"He's fine, Grandma, you don't have to worry about him."

"Oh yes I do!" she sang out. "Your grandpa and I worked hard too, but we knew when to stop. Your daddy never stops.

He's on the go every minute. A person's heart can't take that. And maybe that's why he never laughs anymore. He has to worry all the time, keep up with all the paperwork he's made for himself. Your grandpa and me, we worked for a comfortable life. I never wanted more than that. But your dad, he's never satisfied. I tell him, 'Davy, stop buying, don't you have enough now? What do you want more for? Pay off the homes, pay off your debts, enjoy life while you still can.'"

"He does enjoy life, and he laughs. He loves to laugh, and we love hearing him laugh."

"No, I tell you, he's not the same. He's pushing himself. Is it your mother? Does she want more, always more?" She shook her head as if the verdict were already in.

Ellie blinked with relief when the phone rang. She didn't want to have to take sides in the war between her mother and Lillian. "It's probably Mae," she said, knowing Lillian's younger sister called every morning to ask how things were going with Earl.

Lillian scraped out of the booth to answer the phone fastened to the wall by the dining room door.

Mae lived across town with her husband, Leo, in affordable senior housing. Both of them were obese with multiple health problems, but always eager to see their only nephew, Dave, and any of his children when they visited. They had no children of their own, and the Millers were their closest relatives. Usually, Ellie drove over to their immaculate apartment for an hour's visit, which always made her grand-mother resentful. Lillian disliked sharing her family with her younger sister—her lifelong rival. At one time, they had stopped speaking to each other for five years because Lillian had accused Leo of making a pass at her. Ultimately, Ellie's father had managed to negotiate a truce, but only for a relationship of restrained politeness on Lillian's part. Mae was more softhearted, gregarious, and flexible than Lillian.

Lillian came back to the nook. "You were right—it was Mae. She hopes you'll stop by."

"I can go over tomorrow on my way home," Ellie said.

"Good. That'll please her." She took the last sip in her glass and licked the taste on her lips. "Mae and me, we never got along. Mae always got what she wanted—she was Papa's pet. She was cute and affectionate. He fell for that. I could never be that way. I was smart and argued with him. I wanted to finish high school, I wanted to be my own boss, and that made him angry. He made me go into the family business, while he let Mae go to beauty school and open her own shop. I was closer to my mother and took care of her when she died. I held her in my arms her last hours—oh, I'll never forget!" Her plump arms cradled the memory of her mother close to her body. "I told her, 'Mother, it's all right. Don't be afraid, I'm right here with you.' I watched her take her last breaths." She paused for a moment, lost in the memory.

Ellie studied her face—round, with a redhead's flawless,

creamy skin, not a serious wrinkle showing in her late seventies. That's what made her smile look so angelic. She had a dainty nose, turned slightly down at the tip and flaring back at the nostrils. Her keen blue eyes—so like Dave's—showed calculating intelligence, but her mind lacked worldly education. She loved good times with others, livening up, even getting boisterous. She welcomed the visits of her granddaughters, who told her all about the current lifestyles and trends in Philadelphia—nothing she wanted for herself but liked hearing about. She didn't trust other people when it came to financial transactions, even simple ones at the grocery store. She clutched her black change purse suspiciously before feeling forced to open it. But merrymaking with family and friends was a part of her heritage that offered warmth and the feeling of love and togetherness. And she loved her son. She listened to his advice, and financially they had become partners, though she let him take the lead, as he had learned more about estate planning. When the grandkids were younger, she and Earl came to Philadelphia for Christmas, but she couldn't handle the commotion of so many people—seven of them in that big house. It was too many personalities for Lillian to cope with, and on Jean's turf, not hers. She couldn't have sole access to Dave. She hardly had thirty seconds alone with him, and usually by the kitchen bar when he mixed drinks at five o'clock, for otherwise he was off doing things, always in motion. The holiday commotion also made him uptight, short on patience. Ellie knew her grandmother's sulks and insults during those holidays would have resulted in permanent estrangement, if it hadn't been for her father cajoling her out of them. She would manage goodbye thank yous and kisses, then return home to hibernate for a while, abstaining from corresponding with the granddaughters, but still answering Dave's faithful Sunday calls, when they talked about money and investments. Money was their common ground, what they always did together by phone or in person. Eventually, when the bad blood had subsided, Ellie would call to propose a weekend visit, and Lillian's voice would stammer in relief, "Oh, Ellie, I was just getting ready to call you."

That afternoon, Hen and Myrtle stopped by. Hen was a distant cousin of Lillian's, a few years younger. Lillian led them straight to Earl's bedside. Hen bent his jovial, pockmarked face over the safety rail and said, "Why, howdy there, Earl, how're you doing today?"

Myrtle also leaned in and stroked Earl's white hair. "You're sure lookin' good, Earlie, as handsome as always. We want to see you get well again—back on your feet, you hear?"

Earl's head moved, and his throat croaked in an effort to speak. A choking episode followed that left him panicked to catch his breath. When it finally ended, his head lay limp on the pillow—it was no use, life, free will, was over—forever.

The group around his bed stared in awkward understanding, which made their false cheer, their brightness of hope, impossible to maintain. It was a relief to leave him alone and follow Lillian to the kitchen, the realm of the living. Once more Ellie was aware of how the dining room's wall was a border between the two realms.

"We can only stay a minute," Myrtle said. "We know you have lots to do, Lilly."

"Oh no, not at all—I'm so glad you're here, and Ellie's helping me. I say we celebrate with a highball! How about it? These times are hard—let's remember the good." Her hopeful smile, with bobbing brows and twinkling eyes, forced them to linger in her time of need. If they left, it would be a rejection, cause disappointment, even resentment or a grudge, given Lillian's personality.

"Oh, all right, if you're sure," Myrtle said, after exchanging a helpless look with her husband.

"*Von*-derful!" Lillian said, clapping her hands. "Ellie, could you make us some highballs?"

"Sure, tell me how."

Lillian chortled. "Why that's easy, darling—whiskey and soda over ice—and no skimping on the whiskey, and just a splash of soda. Use the taller glasses. Now come sit down, yous all, just like old times. I'm so glad you came to see Earl— it cheers him up. If only he could be with us now."

The visit soon became lively with the highballs going

down. Ellie had one too and appreciated the immediate high—the escape from the tedium of being alone with Lillian. And yet, she came for these visits voluntarily, for Lillian was family for her own loneliness.

Lillian was now bubbling away with exaggerated praise for Ellie. "I couldn't do any of this without her help, she's been a godsend! And Hen, she's interested in our family's history. She takes notes when we talk. You have to help her. You know much more about our family than me. Ask Hen all your questions, Ellie." She winked at her cousin. "Ellie's a writer like me."

Ellie smiled and nodded, despite wondering about the comparison. It was true, though, that her grandmother liked to write letters, and now and then they contained a verse—the rhyming, sentimental kind on greeting cards. Maybe it was true that a strain of her grandmother's ear for music had come down to Ellie in the way of words, their sound in her ears.

Dutifully, she asked Hen a few questions about the family tree, but his knowledge quickly turned out to be as limited as Lillian's, and the subject petered out. However, it led the elders to happy recollections of their youth—their times and culture so different from Ellie's, with the '60s and '70s social and sexual revolutions.

"We had to hide everything we did with our boyfriends," Lillian said, "like finding a way to meet without a chaperone. We had to sneak."

"Not like today," Hen laughed. "I would've had me a ball if I was a boy today!"

Lillian burst out laughing. "Don't you know it—we had rules for everything!"

"But we sure managed to find ways to break 'em!" Hen said.

"Remember Carl and Ruby? Don't tell me you forget what happened to them!"

"Hmm, better remind me," Hen said.

"Canoe rides, does that ring a bell?"

"Oh, yeah, those two were always setting off on canoe rides!" Hen laughed.

Lillian jumped from the booth and slapped her thigh in hilarity. "And that's why they had to hurry up and get married! Think of it—the two of them in the canoe managing that." She chortled—this was racy! The others half-laughed along with her. Then, she slid back into her seat. "It was easier for you boys. But girls like me were watched by their fathers. I had a hard time of it. What about you, Myrtle? Could you sneak out for a good time with Hen?" Lillian's eyes glittered in the hopes of another juicy story, one that might finally be revealed, given the liberal times.

But her prompting was a conversation stopper. Myrtle's lips sealed tight, and Hen's laughter died out with a sigh, eyes going down.

Ellie quickly changed the subject. "Do you live nearby? Do you have kids and grandkids in town?"

Myrtle was happy to tell Ellie about their daughter, now grown and living in Chicago. The grandkids were in college, so it wasn't often they all got together. "We aren't as lucky as Lillian with all you grandkids visiting," Myrtle said. "But lookee here, I always carry a few pictures in my purse." She got them out to share.

The hour wore on, the peak effect of the highball wore off, and the get-together came to a pleasant close, everyone ready to hug and say goodbye, with repeated well wishes and intentions to meet again soon. Standing on the threshold of the swinging dining room door, Hen and Myrtle bid a cheerful goodbye to Earl, everyone aware it might be the last time they saw him alive.

A few days later, Earl died. Lillian told Ellie the details over the phone. "He choked on his phlegm—oh my God, it was horrible. I'm glad you weren't here to see it. I called 911, and a nurse came. She had that thing that sucks the mucus out. But he was too frail. After she got him breathing again, I went with her to the door, and that's when he died. Oh, Lordy! He was gone when I came back." Her voice sailed away with the memory.

The following weekend, Ellie's family gathered at the hillside home for Earl's funeral. They arrived in separate cars, for the girls lived independently and Jay was still at home with their parents. He was fifteen now, good-looking, and as carefree as always. He had been born before the feminist movement, before Laurie and Ellie challenged their father's sexism. They had laughed along whenever Dave's eyes twinkled at them that now, finally, the family had "family jewels" to pass on. Ellie had never asked Laurie if Jay's birth had filled her with relief from the shame of being born a girl and a disappointment to their parents. Or, perhaps, Ellie— being the second girl—had been the greater disappointment. And Laurie was different. She was naturally headstrong, bold. In college, she had become a vocal feminist and was now halfway through medical school, determined to outdistance their father. She and Ellie were still sisterly, but their lives had taken different paths—Laurie the achiever and Ellie the shy and insecure writer.

After Jay's birth, Ellie's mother had blossomed into a happier person—no more rages. She loved social life, dressing up and fulfilling the role she had been raised to achieve—the wife and envied beauty of a successful man. This was also what her husband wanted—an enviable ornament on his arm. Unconsciously, Jean leaned on Laurie with her Main Line education and friends to dictate the latest lifestyle trends essential for the family's outward appearance. Ellie's cohort wasn't Main Line but more the fringe. Now, with Jay soon to leave the nest, Jean was thinking about her future, how to fill her days. Laurie told her to get a job—she could teach, she had already taught first grade briefly before getting married—she could go back to it. At a recent family dinner, with her daughters home for the meal, Jean had playfully broached the topic of taking courses for a teaching certificate. Dave had vehemently opposed it—their friends would think he couldn't support his wife! Laurie had argued back like a defense attorney, and Ellie had agreed with her. Jay, when asked his opinion, had shrugged benignly—"Mom should do what she wants." Jean—now supported unanimously by her children—had sat back with a pleased smile. She knew in a day or two Dave would grudgingly concede.

The dining room had been cleared of the hospital equipment and restored to its formal mid-century decor. The family hung out there because of the table and chairs and the picture window's view. The room's high perch overlooking nature lessened the claustrophobia of dealing with death and a funeral. Despite the somber occasion and Dr. Dave's pale, strained face, the family's usual excitement of being together enlivened the atmosphere. Jay was their pivotal point, generating fun and laughter, despite his left arm being in a plaster cast, the result of a daredevil skateboard trick.

On the day of the funeral, Mrs. Miller's dress pumps could be heard tapping on the old wood staircase as she came down. Ellie and her siblings waited for her in the dining room, annoyed at her lateness. Their father and grandmother were already at the funeral parlor greeting guests without the rest of the family there for support. But Mrs. Miller was always late, always dawdling over her appearance in order to delay the moment of presenting herself to others and seeing their stares and judgment. Even now, with her own kids, she was all nerves and chattered in a fluttery voice on the stairs just to let them know she was about to enter—but the warning was more for herself than for them. At last, she stepped into the archway, a proscenium framing her hourglass figure in a dark purple suit. She had been to the hairdresser the day before and her blond sheen cupped her pretty face. Her tasteful jewelry, the gift of her husband, marked her social status. Although she always nearly panicked to face other people's stares, she also dressed for that very effect—the effect of her beauty. It had been the browbeaten cornerstone of her upbringing.

"Grandma must be getting pissed we're late," she said lightly.

"You mean you're late," Laurie said.

The phone rang, and Jay leaped to the kitchen wall to answer it.

"I dread this," Ellie said. "Who wants to see Grandpa all madeup and looking fake?"

"We're doing it for Grandma," Mrs. Miller said. "We

might not want open caskets ourselves, but this is what she wants. And it's probably what everyone expects around here."

"Hey, Ma," Jay called from the swinging door, holding the phone's receiver in his good hand. "Grandma wants to know where we are."

"Oh, dear, tell her we're leaving right now. Come on, kids, let's go. Who's driving?"

"Me, but I need directions," Laurie said.

Blank faces stared at her.

"Wait, Jay! Don't hang up! We need directions!" Ellie said.

"I hung up."

"Shit!" Mrs. Miller said. *Shit* was her new, favorite word, now that the liberal times allowed women of her ilk to say it, as well as other once-forbidden words.

Laurie pursed her lips and turned to Ellie. "Did Daddy tell you the name of the funeral home?"

"No."

She glared at her mother—the last person on earth to know. "Ma?"

"Well … he might have mentioned … no, I didn't hear what he said."

"You mean you didn't listen," Laurie said.

"Let's go," Ellie said. "Maybe her church knows—it's down the street."

Eventually, they made it to the funeral parlor, passing

through streets of a vernacular architecture—row houses with little pointed towers running entire blocks. Stone churches anchored heavily to many corners. All had become shabby, the town's golden century in the past.

Greeters in black suits ushered them into a dark, windowless room smelling of candles and disinfectants. Large vases of flowers added another, almost sour odor to the room, as if death and the underworld dwelled there. A few rows of chairs had been set up in one half of the room, and a handful of white-haired people from Lillian's church and circle of friends sat there. They stared at the newcomers—obviously city folk by the way they dressed. Mae and Leo sat in the front row next to Hen and Myrtle, the only relatives left in Lillian's line. Earl had no line that they knew of. The Millers hugged the relatives and smiled with nods at the other guests, but didn't linger by the chairs. They moved to the other half of the room with the open casket, where Lillian, Dr. Miller, and the pastor stood greeting an older couple who had just arrived. Ellie noticed how the couple shook hands courteously with the family but warmed up with Dr. Miller, whom they called Doc. He was a member of their clan, most of them having known him in his youth, through his Boy Scout and high school years. They were proud of him, proud that their hometown boy had risen so high in the world beyond their borders.

Lillian was hardly recognizable. She had dressed up in

a navy-blue suit and low black heels, her posture straight and proud. She wore makeup that brightened her visage, and Mae had cut and curled her hair early that morning. She looked poised and self-assured of her place in this community. She didn't need Dave to preside over the occasion—this was her event, and he was her supporting son.

Laurie and Mrs. Miller stayed close to Dave, while Ellie and Jay hesitantly approached the casket.

"Jeez," Jay said, "this is weird—he looks fake ... but maybe alive."

Ellie stared with the same unease at what the undertaker had created. Earl's chiseled cheekbones, forthright nose, and sealed eyes faced the ceiling under layers of undetectable makeup that resulted in a wax museum face. The white hair—the only natural thing about him besides his black eyelashes—was brushed back beautifully from the unreal face. One look was enough for her. "Come on," she said, nudging Jay's shoulder toward Laurie and their parents. The pastor and Lillian had moved away to talk to the seated guests.

"Hi Daddy," Ellie said, giving her father a hug. "How are you doing?"

"I'm okay. I've had a lot of time to get ready for this, so don't worry about me," he said quietly.

But his face was drawn and ashen. His heavy drinking the night before had left him with droopy jowls and puffy eyelids. Nevertheless, his dark hair and distinguished carriage lent him stature.

"I want to thank you for being with Grandma last weekend—and other weekends—she's mentioned it several times—how supportive you've been," he said.

"I wanted to be here—I loved Grandpa, I still do."

"I know, but thank you, and also for your poem." He patted his suit coat's breast pocket. "I read it, and I want you to know it means a lot to me."

Her heart leaped hearing that her poem had pleased him. It gave a lasting life to Earl—to his soul—for both of them.

Dr. Miller turned to Jay and patted his shoulder. "How's the arm, big guy?" he said quietly.

"Fucking broken, Dad—whadda ya think?" Jay said.

"Listen, try to watch your language around here—these people are older and more conservative, but they care, that's why they're here, and they deserve our respect."

"Okay, but they didn't hear me."

"Just watch it, that's all."

Laurie and Mrs. Miller moved closer.

"Dad, did you know Grandma bought three cemetery plots—one for you too?" Laurie said.

"Yes, she mentioned it once, but I told her I don't plan to use it, and she should sell it."

"But Dad, she bought them after you got married. She left Mom out."

"Okay, let's not talk about that now. The plots aren't of interest to me. Grandma's Grandma, just accept how she is. She means well."

"Oh, ho ho," Mrs. Miller said.

Dr. Miller put a comforting arm around her back to show whose side he was on.

Jay looked up from the printed program he had been skimming. "It says here Grandpa was a Mason. What's that, Dad?"

"I don't know much about them, or Dad's involvement, but I believe he joined because he was a master printer. They're a secret society—like a brotherhood with meetings and rituals," Dr. Miller said.

"You mean a cult?"

"No, just a club of men committed to good values. Hey, listen, I want to reiterate, these are good people here—neighbors, friends—please show respect."

"Yah," Jay said, and moved away. Ellie followed him. At family gatherings, they often stuck together.

"Want to check the outdoors?" Jay said.

"Yeah, air."

"Got any cigs?"

"No, I quit."

"Again?"

"Hey kids," Dr. Miller called quietly after them. "Don't stray too far, we go to the cemetery next."

Several hours later, they said goodbye to the last sprinkling of friends and relatives who had come back to the house for sandwiches and drinks. Life was now ready to go on, the funeral over. Lillian and Dave settled in the nook to read Earl's will. Mrs. Miller and Jay sat together on the living room couch to pore over old photos and memorabilia from the stuffed closet. Laurie went upstairs to study her medical texts, and Ellie went out for a walk on Egelman Road. The street was quiet, few cars used it, though she had grown up knowing how dangerous it could be—a toddler had once wandered out and been killed. The neighborhood was one of working folk, with young men tinkering under their car hoods on weekends. Laundry flapped from clotheslines and the sound of TVs came through the closed windows of nondescript houses. Ellie tried to imagine her father growing up here, and what it was like to have a vision that went beyond it, and to take, independently, all the steps that led out of it. And how she, as a result, had grown up in a completely different culture, one of privilege.

That evening the family gathered for dinner in the dining room—a last supper before everyone went their separate ways in the morning. Ellie knew it would be hard for her grandmother to be all alone, and yet, she would be all right. Even if she padded around in a daze for a while—even if she sipped beer before five o'clock until her self-discipline returned—she would still have purpose living inside her, financial purpose. She would start thinking about the summer ahead, when she could resume her stimulating rental activities on the Jersey Shore, where she took satisfaction in earning her entire year's living expenses in three short months. She loved taking in money, especially cash, and counting it, licking her thumb every so often to separate the bills.

Ellie and Laurie made dinner—Laurie in charge. In the fridge, they found chicken, green beans, and a big jar of Lillian's pepper hash—a sweet-and-sour slaw. When they sat down to eat and Jay helped himself to the vegetables, his eyes twinkled at his grandmother—"Well, whadda ya know kiddos, we're having *wedge-tables* for dinner."

Lillian roared with laughter, the kind that couldn't stop but just fed more. The others joined in. "Don't you know it!" Lillian finally gasped, wiping tears from her face. "That's how we talk in these parts. Davy, pour me some more wine, would you please?" she said, holding up her glass to Dave at the other end of the table.

The wine and beer had been flowing all evening—French wine Dave had brought from his own cellar, knowing his mother only offered purple stuff from an open gallon jug that had sat on the cellar stairs for years. Soon, Grandma was howling with enjoyment, purging her weeks and months of stress, turning them into hilarity with the family, even with her nemesis—Jean—who was also laughing and joking with abandon.

Raising her voice to be heard above the din, Lillian said, "I have a story for yous all."

Flushed and shining faces turned to her.

"You'd think I deserved just one day of peace after Earl passed, but no sirree, that wasn't in the cards. Those boys from Schneiders no sooner came for Earl's body, than another boy knocked on my door. I opened it just a crack to let him know I was in mourning. 'Mr. Miller died this morning, you'll have to come back another time.' He apologized for disturbing me. 'I'm Frankie Getz, I think you know my mother,' he said. 'I'm getting married next month and want to buy a silver set.' 'Wait,' I told him, 'come on in, I'll show you the patterns.' You see, his mama's been real good to me—she works on the *Gazette* and sends me customers."

"Always ready to make a deal, Grandma!" Jay teased.

Lillian chortled and wagged a finger at him. "Darn right, sonny boy! And your daddy learned it from me. Am I right, Davy?"

From the other end of the table, Dave nodded but with a detached smile. Ellie thought he was the only one who couldn't forget their recent loss.

"Is it true, Grandma, what Laurie said, that you bought Daddy a house here when he graduated from medical school?" Jay asked.

Her face lit up. "Indeed we did! We thought he'd take a job at one of our hospitals, but oh no, your daddy had much bigger plans for yous all!" Her red brows bobbed as her eyes circled the table. "And we had found the perfect place—it had four bedrooms right on Doctors' Row."

Ellie hadn't heard that story before. And it was the first time she'd heard of Doctor's Row. She would have to follow up on her next visit—do a drive by.

"*Vell,*" Lillian said, taking a deep breath. "Isn't this just *von*-derful! Earl's gone, but here we are—we're still a family. And Grandpa's not really gone, he's with us, he'll always be with us. Why, I can feel him right now—he's here in this room. Can you feel it?"

The others weren't sure how to answer.

But Lillian was oblivious to them, her eyes rising to the ceiling. "Why hello there, Earlie, we're so happy you're with us tonight—oh my darling, we're all together, forever!" Her eyes came back down and circled the table with her angelic smile. "Let's all hold hands," she said. "We might not be all that religious in this family, but we're just as thankful for what we've got."

They granted her wish and hesitantly joined hands, for holding hands at the table was something the younger

Millers associated with prayer, which wasn't part of their household. But this wasn't about prayer or religion, Ellie thought, it was about family and being together. And maybe that was like religion, or pure religion without a church— just the individual's soul connected to something intangible beyond the body and mind.

"Yes, indeed," Lillian sang in her soprano voice, "I'm so thankful for all of you. We're family, we have our differences, but we always manage to get through our ups and downs. We forgive and stick together. We know how to love each other, and that's what matters." A sneaky smile then twinkled in her eyes. "And don't any of you ever forget, I'm still the head of this family!" She released the hands she held and blew happy kisses at all of them. Then, she raised her glass in salute to her descendants. Automatically they lifted theirs to her.

Book design by Jeremy Eberts

Bergamot Books, www. bergamotbooks.com